# DOG DIARIES

## STEVEN BUTLER
## AND JAMES PATTERSON

Illustrated by
RICHARD WATSON

1 3 5 7 9 10 8 6 4 2

Young Arrow
20 Vauxhall Bridge Road
London SW1V 2SA

Young Arrow is part of the Penguin Random House group of companies
whose addresses can be found at global.penguinrandomhouse.com

Penguin
Random House
UK

Copyright © James Patterson 2018
Illustrations by Richard Watson

James Patterson has asserted his right to be identified as the author of this
Work in accordance with the Copyright, Designs and Patents Act 1988

First published by Young Arrow in 2018

www.penguin.co.uk

A CIP catalogue record for this book is available from the British Library

ISBN 9781784759629

Printed and bound in Great Britain by
Clays Ltd, St Ives Plc

Penguin Random House is committed to a sustainable future for our
business, our readers and our planet. This book is made from Forest
Stewardship Council® certified paper.

*For Michelle, Dizzy and Odie – my park pals*
*– S.B.*

OOOOOH! You opened it! You actually opened my book!

I've been waiting for ages, and now a human-youngling is finally reading the beginning of my story.

This is a waggy-tail-icious moment! I don't think I've been this excited since… since…since I spotted a raccoon out by the trash cans and chased it up a fence!

That was a good day…IT WAS,TERRIFIC… one of the greatest, but this is even greater!

I love humans, and I bet you're a really tremendous one.

Oh boy, oh boy, oh boy!

Okay, I need to calm down a little if we're going to get this story told.

Hmmm…what to do first?

Oh yeah! Here's a gift just for you. It'd be rude of me not to share my best-best-BEST treasure.

MY FAVOURITE STICK!

It's yours, I insist. One end is a little chewed, but the rest of it is excellent. Don't crunch it all at once.

There—now you're my really real person-pal and we can start the story properly.

Sit!

Sit!

Down!

Ha ha...I've always wanted to say that to a human.

Okay. If you're all comfortable, I'll begin...

I remember it like it was yesterday.

The happiest moment of a mutt's life, when you see your pet human for the first time, and you know instantly that you're going to be BEST FRIENDS forever.

That's how it was when I met mine, and OH BOY do I have a great pet. But I'm getting ahead of myself. You don't even know who I am.

I should probably start this story the way

you humans like to, with an introduction. Us pooches don't normally bother with things like that. We usually prefer to take a polite sniff of each other's butts and—HEY PRESTO!—we're sorted with all the information we need. But for you, my non-furry reader, I'll make an exception.

My name is Junior—hello! Or should I say, HERROOOOOOOOOOOOOOOOOW?

If you hadn't guessed already, I'm a dog. Yep…shiny-nosed…licky-tongued…floppy-eared…bow-wow-woof-woof…and you're holding my daily doggy diary in your five fingery digits.

Consider yourself extremely lucky, my person-pal. In this book, you'll find the story of my life so far with my brand-new family, and it's a HUMDINGER!

Now, I know what you're thinking. You're sat there, wrinkling up your forehead as we speak, saying "A dog's diary?" to yourself and picturing my furry little paws typing away at a computer or scribbling in a notebook. Don't be so people-brained…Ha!

You may also be wondering why on earth I would be keeping a journal. That's what princesses locked in towers, or grandmoos and grand-paws get up to, right?

WRONG!

In case you didn't know, all canines keep diaries. IT'S TRUE! We always have, ever since the DAWN OF DOG…all the way back to the time of the cavepeople and their saber-toothed terriers…

Just not in the same way that humans might.

Why do you think we all stop to sniff
every corner and streetlight and fire hydrant
on our morning walk?

Never thought about it, huh?

Well, I'll tell you.

We're snooping on the local gossip, checking who's been around, and generally keeping up to date with what's happening in the neighborhood. To us, having a good snuffle is like reading the news.

You see, dogs keep smell diaries. Every pee and poop tells a tale, dontchaknow? But let's not panic just yet. I'm not about to ask you to stop and sniff my…ummm…you-know-what.

Nope, with the help of some booky brainiac humans, my story has been written down. Incredible, huh? They can do ANYTHING nowadays. And you can safely enjoy every word without having to worry about all the whiffs and stinks. IT'S EXCELLENT! EVERYBODY WINS!

So, where was I?

Oh, yeah, my pet human. I guess the day I came to live with him and his family is the best place to begin my diary. It's my happiest day of them all, so far.

Only last year, my life was a seriously different bowl of kibble.

Like so many of my furry friends, I was serving life in the slammer…the clink… pooch prison!

You guessed it. My luck had run out and I found myself locked away in the scariest place in the whole world. Scratch that— THE WHOLE UNIVERSE!

# HILLS VILLAGE DOG SHELTER!

There are no ear scratches or belly rubs or nose boops in that place, let me tell you. No siree! The humans who work there shuffle past, ignoring you, and don't even want to play ball! I KNOW! IT'S HORRIFIC!

That place is one great big boredom-fest. It's enough to turn even the bounciest pup into a small globule of glum in no time. BUT...I'm not there now, ha ha!

Yipp-yipp-yippee, I can't wait to tell you this part.

Alrighty. Do you have spare snacks to keep us both happy as we scamper through the next few pages together?

You do?

EXCELLENT!

# The First Day:
# A Lot of Tuesdays Ago...

I was sitting in the backyard of a house with the old lady called Grandmoo who smells like ointment and bug spray, the Mom-Lady, and the little one with a voice like a dog whistle staring down at me.

Mom-Lady had collected me from the shelter earlier that day, and it was all SO EXCITING! She bought me a new green

~~GRANDMA~~
Grandmoo

~~MOM~~
Mom-Lady

~~GEORGIA~~
Jawjaw

**13**

collar with a jingly tag on it, and I got to ride up front in one of those moving people-boxes on wheels. I had to concentrate really hard so I didn't pee on the seats with happiness.

Later, though, we were just waiting around for something, I guess…or someone. It seemed to go on forever and was very confusing.

I looked up at the three different-sized ladies and tried to figure out what they were thinking about. I'd been hoping for a treat or two and was even trying out my best puppy-dog eyes on the oldest one, but so far it hadn't worked.

The littlest person (her name is Jawjaw) was complaining and grumbling because she said I was going to mess up her room.

What room? We were in the yard! At this point, my understanding of the Peoplish language was pretty crummy, but I could tell she wasn't happy with me. I wagged my tail and jumped up a few times, leaving muddy paw-prints on her knees (humans LOVE that), but she pushed me away, grunting.

*This can't be it*, I thought to myself. *It's just like the shelter. No one wants to play.*

But…one person did…

"Hey!" a boy's voice shouted from inside the house.

Mom-Lady called to it, and a skinny kid with messy hair and long, gangly legs clomped out through the back door.

That was it! That was the moment I laid eyes on my pet human for the first time. It makes my tail go crazy just remembering it.

"Surprise!" shouted Mom-Lady.

"Is that…?" my pet human gasped. He looked completely shocked, like he'd just swallowed a hornet's nest.

"It's a dog!" Grandmoo said.

"Well, yeah," mumbled my pet human, "but does he…?"

Jawjaw grumbled about something again. I was beginning to think I didn't like her all that much. She certainly didn't like me.

"I mean, is he…mine?" my pet human asked.

"Yes," said Mom-Lady. "He's yours, Ruff."

RUFF! The best-best-BESTEST name in all the world.

Before I knew it, Ruff was down on the ground and I was planting as many slobbery licks on his cheek as I could. He smelled like junk food and broken rules, and his face tasted like mischief. I loved all of it. They say you never adore anything as much as your first pet, and I couldn't agree more.

Don't get me wrong—I'd known plenty of other humans back before I wound up in the dog shelter, but none of those were mine to keep.

Finally I had a buddy for life. Just look at him…

RAFE ~~KHATCHA~~DORIAN

RUFF CATCH-A-DOGGY-BONE

His full name is Ruff Catch-A-Doggy-Bone. I know! What are the odds a human would have such a poochish name!?!

He smiled down at me, and I jumped about his legs, nipping and bouncing and yipping. It's what us dogs call "The Happy Dance."

Hey…don't judge. I was having the time of my little life, and once you've finished this book, you'll be Happy-Dancing all over the place, I'll bet.

Anyway, just when I thought things couldn't get any better…any more

TERRIFICALLY WONDERFUL,

Ruff said the two most magical words I think ever existed.

They're so powerful, these words can leave you wagging your tail for days.

Agh! I'm not sure I can even tell you what he said, it makes me so overexcited.

Okay…breathe, Junior.

Breathe in…

Breathe out…

Breathe in…

Breathe out…

Right, I'm ready.

Ruff looked down at me.

He smiled his goofy human smile, then patted me on the head, opened his mouth…and said it…

HE JUST SAID IT!

GOOD BOY!

I swear, I could have exploded into a billion little doggy pieces at that moment. Someone was telling me I was a GOOD BOY!

So there it is...the beginning of my story. We're on page 22 and you're still here reading with me. I knew you would be. Great, isn't it? Well, there's plenty more to tell you, so don't go anywhere just yet.

My life with the Catch-A-Doggy-Bone family had finally begun, and it's all fun and games from here on out in our BRILLIANT home.

Come and see if you don't believe me...

## Today...Friday:
## The Catch-A-Doggy-Bone
## Kennel

Okay...if I tell the story properly...like PROPERLY-PROPERLY...you stand to learn quite a lot from my BRILLIANT diary. I'd say every human in the world could use a few tips on how to live a little bit more like us pooches. After all, who's happier than a dog?

Think of this book as a MUTT MANUAL...
CANINE CLASS...DROOL SCHOOL...and
you'll be enjoying a more SMELL-TASTIC life
in no time.

Let's start with a wander around my home.
It's not as big and whiffly as some of the
enormous kennels over on the far side of
town, but for the Catch-A-Doggy-Bone
pack, it's just right.

Our family kennel is warm and cozy, and
FULL of all the things a dog needs to get
by—when you know where to look.

Now, if you're going to live just like
a MASTERFUL MUTT, you need to learn
all the coolest hiding places, things to
sniff, spots to stash your snacks
and toys (a pooch's life is not

worth living without those), escape routes, and vantage points for barking at people walking through your neighborhood. You name it, I'll teach you where to find it.

If your kennel is anything like mine, it'll be stuffed full of all these and more.

C'mon…I'll show you the best bits.

# The Sleep Room

A pet human's sleep room is practically a jungle gym to us dogs. It's filled from top to bottom with amazing things to taste and smell and play with, and where all the best hugs and scratches happen. Let's not forget it's also the one place in the whole kennel where little brothers and sisters almost never dare to tread…almost. Treats hidden in here are safest from sniffing snouts and snooping eyes.

## The Food Room

**N**o human kennel is complete without a great big room filled with FOOD! It's the yummiest, smelliest, most snack-tastic place to be.

Just by luck, Mom-Lady keeps the broom in the same cupboard as all the bags and boxes of my treats.

I figured it out ages ago…the more mess I make, the more she opens the cupboard, giving me the chance to snaffle a few Crunchy-Lumps or Doggo-Drops. Ha ha! I'm a genius…what can I say?

Ah, food…sigh!

## The Rainy Poop Room

This room is so weird! Whoever heard of a room just for pooping and washing? That's what backyards are for! Humans can be so funny at times…but hey…if you don't judge me for my Happy Dance, I won't judge you guys and your rainy poop rooms.

# The Picture Box Room

The Picture Box Room is where humans love to sit and stare for hours. It's a real puzzle to me…

It's the one room of the kennel that has a perfect view of the street, which makes it a great barking base, and I keep my most delicious treats under the big hairy square on the floor. VERY IMPORTANT!

## Jawjaw's Room

**J**awjaw's Room is strictly out of bounds whenever she's at home, but the rooms you aren't supposed to go in are always the most interesting. Her shoes are by far the most delicious, but watch out for her army of mini-humans—they see everything!

## The Backyard

The backyard is my little kingdom. It's extremely important that I protect it by barking at birds, squirrels, RACCOONS, airplanes, RACCOONS, clouds, neighbors, RACCOONS, and moving people-boxes on wheels…

AND RACCOONS!

## Then there's one last place...

**B**race yourself, my person-pal! I didn't want to have to show you this, but I have no choice. If your kennel is just like mine, there is one spot in your home that's more scary, more dangerous, MORE TERRIFYING than any other.

Don't turn the page until you've hidden yourself safely away. GO!!

**40**

RUUUUUNNNNNNNN!!! Take my book with you and hide.

Under the bed! In the laundry pile! BEHIND THE COMFY SQUISHY THING!

Are you safe in your secret spot?

Okay…the most spine-jangling place in the house is…

Don't get me wrong, it's not the closet itself that's horrifying. It's what lives in there…

Lurking in the shadows among the coats and winter boots is a monster that would turn a Dalmatian's spots white with terror. It's my archest of enemies, and has gobbled up some of my most precious treasures in the past.

Inside that cupboard of doom lives…

THE VACUUM CLEANER!

It's the most evil creature I've ever met and it always comes out to roar around the house when Ruff and Jawjaw are at school. Mom-Lady pushes and pulls it through the rooms in a terrible battle of strength. It's hard to tell who's winning sometimes as it's sucking and slobbering up all the best pieces of breakfast from the floor, but eventually Mom-Lady always defeats it by unplugging its tail from the wall.

For instance—this morning, I'd spent ages gathering all my stashed treats and piling them together under the rug in the Picture Box Room. It was a mouthwatering masterpiece...and, you guessed it...just as I turned my back and headed off for a nap in Jawjaw's Room, the Vacuum Cleaner starts growling...then, *kapow!*

I barely made it to the Picture Box Room door before that monster had gulped up my entire store. It was heartbreaking. I hid under Ruff's bed and whimpered to myself for hours after that.

He only managed to coax me out this evening with the promise of a fresh Denta-Toothy-Chew and one of his AMAZING belly rubs…

## 10 p.m.

**W**ell, now you've learned all about the wins and outs of the Catch-A-Doggy-Bone kennel, I feel like we're really getting to know each other.

Ruff brought a big bowl of Tripple-Yummo-Banana-Twist ice cream to bed with him tonight, and now I'm curled up by his feet, watching him eat it as he doodles in his doodle pad.

My pet loves to draw. He's even drawn me a few times.

I'm just going to keep quiet for now, though, and let Ruff finish his ice cream. He normally dozes off pretty soon after…

Then I can lick the bowl. HA HA!

# Saturday

## 6:12 a.m.

**W**ake up! Wake up! Wake up!
Today is one of the two special days per week when Ruff doesn't go to school. They're my favorite! I get to spend two whole days with my best pet-pal and we can do whatever we want...and I mean anything!

I've had a good think about all the fun stuff I want to tick off the list, but it's so difficult to choose what to do first.

I definitely want to try out some new napping spots around the kennel, and of course I have to wait for the mailman to come (he loves it when I bark at him from the Picture Box Room window), and there's an unchewed table leg in the Food Room that I've been meaning to take care of for weeks.

A dog's work is never done...

I guess I should wake up Ruff. Normally I do it as soon as the sun rises (he LOVES it when I do that), but I let him sleep in a little later today. I'll just go stand on his face for a second.

Every good dog knows there's no nicer way for a human to be woken than with a paw-poke in the center of their forehead.

I won't be a mo…

## 10 a.m.

**A**nd we're off, my person-pal…

After a quick game of bite-the-sock while Ruff was getting dressed, our usual breakfast of waffles and maple syrup for the humans and a bowl of CANINE CRISPY CRACKERS for me, we finally decided to go to the dog park.

It's one of the best bits about mornings in the Catch-A-Doggy-Bone kennel.

We have a very set routine…

**1.** Ruff goes to the hallway closet to grab my leash, while I growl from a safe distance to let the Vacuum Cleaner know it can't make a dash for my other secret snack stashes around the kennel.

**2.** Ruff stands in the middle of the hallway, holding my leash, and I do the Happy Dance around his feet. This part is VERY important.

**3.** Once the performance is finished, I let Ruff connect the leash to my collar and I give it a few safety chews, just to make sure it's on there correctly.

**4.** Ruff opens the kennel door and I check the coast is clear of RACCOONS!

**5.** LET WALKIES COMMENCE!

I should tell you that I NEVER go out without my leash on. That way I know my pet human is holding tight and won't get lost when I'm leading him about. I've heard horror stories of careless dogs losing their person-pals and having to bark all over town just to find them. It's awful!

So, only once I know Ruff is safely attached on the other end of my leash do I allow him to head off through the neighborhood.

It's very important that I investigate everybody we pass with a quick jump-up to leave my paw-prints on their knees. It's my stamp of approval. That way, they know I've given them my permission and they're allowed on our street.

Oh…and there are all the SUPER-SERIOUS SNIFFING SPOTS we have to visit on the way. OBVIOUSLY!

## 10:28 a.m.

I can't wait to show you around the park, my furless friend. It's one of the best places in all of Hills Village, and for a super-good reason…

IT'S HOWL-TASTIC!

It's the perfect pooch playground, full of opportunities to cause a bit of chaos, meet your pooch-pals, and make loads of noise.

Yep…once you've peed on the gate, you can head inside the park knowing you're about to have the time of your life in the NOISIEST, SNIFFLEST, GO-CATCH-A-FRISBEE-EST place you'll find for miles and miles around.

There are dogs and their pet humans everywhere!

Fountains to run in and out of…The most talented dogs can run back and forth through the water jets without getting even a teensy bit wet!

The bushes are filled with hundreds of lost tennis balls from past games of fetch that went wrong, and the grass is stuffed full of dropped treats from the doggy obedience classes that happen every evening. Ha! Whoever heard of an obedient dog?

The sticks are the stickiest you've EVER seen, and there are more pigeons than you could ever chase in a squillion years.

All in all, I'd say Hills Village Park is just about the most fun place you could hope

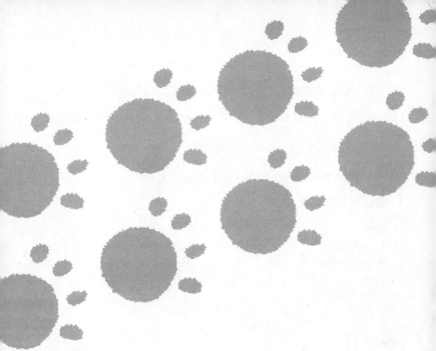

to visit, and it's made even more BRILLIANT
when my friends are also out, taking their
humans for WALKIES.

My pooch-pack are awesome…

Don't get me wrong, people-pals are the
most tremendous thing a dog could wish
for, but you can't get by without some furry
friends too.

This raggle-taggle bunch are my best-best-BESTEST mutt-mates. They're my sniffing squad! My Barking Bunch! MY PLAYTIME PACK!

HA!

## A Quick History of Us...

These guys and I have been through a whole lot together. We met all the way back in our days at the Hills Village Dog Shelter. It was the six of us in one pen for what seemed like forever.

On those long days when things were at their bleakest and a bowl of Meaty-Giblet-Jumble-Chum seemed a lifetime away, we always took care of each other. It was in that horrible place that we swore…

Then one day, a kind-faced lady with more treats in her pockets than we could have imagined in our wildest dreams came and adopted Odin and Diego. They'd always been together since they were pups, and had somehow still not figured out they weren't brothers. But, hey…they believed it, and no one had the heart to tell them there wasn't much of a family resemblance.

Sure enough, once Odin and Diego were saved, one by one all my cellmates were too. Lola went next, followed by Genghis, then Betty, until I was the only loser left in that miserable prison. I remember crying myself to sleep at night, thinking nobody would ever want me and I'd never see any of my friends again. It was horrible!

Fast-forward to six months later. I was feeling about as gloomy and dejected as a mutt could be, so you can imagine my shock and delight when Mom-Lady came to pick me up.

*Finally*, I remember thinking to myself. *Finally, my luck has changed.* I'd never been so happy, and thought my life couldn't possibly get any better…until the day Ruff brought me to the park.

I was a little nervous. I hadn't been around this many dogs before, without metal bars separating us, and seeing so many of them bounding about made me miss my furry friends so much it hurt my heart.

Anyway…to cut a long story short, Ruff and I had only just made it out onto the playing field for a game of fetch when a wiry chihuahua trotted across my path.

My doggy eyes nearly jumped out of my head with surprise. I couldn't believe what I was seeing!

All the hairs on the back of my neck prickled on end as Diego froze in his tracks. He sniffed the air then spun around in my direction.

For a second we both just stared, until…

"Mi amigo!" he barked. "MI AMIGO!"

He practically flew at my face and swung on my left ear. Then we rolled around in the grass, yipping and nipping at each other.

"Mi amigo!" he kept yelping as he play-bit me on my snout. "My old friend, returned?!?!"

**70**

My tail was swishing from side to side so fast I nearly batted the poor little guy across the field like a four-legged baseball.

Next thing I knew, Diego arched his spine, lifted his head, and HOOOOOOOWLED!

HEEEEEEE'SSSSS BAAAAACK!!

"HOOOOOOOOOWWWWLLLLLL!"
came another voice from the other side of
the field.

"OOOOW-OOOOW-
OOOOOOOOOW!" a third voice wailed
from the fountains.

"BAAAA-WUUUUUUHHHHHH!"

"YIP-YIP-YIIIIIIIIIIIIIIIIIIIP!"

And that was that—I turned around
slowly to see all my best pooch-pals
running toward me from
all different directions.

Needless to say...
IT WAS A GOOD DAY!

There's not a whole lot I
can say that properly describes
just how great these guys are.

Odin and Diego are endlessly funny. You should see it when Diego scampers beneath something low, like a trash can or a bench, and Odin can't figure out why he's not able to make it under like his brother... ha ha!

Lola lives to roll in mud. She's more hippopotamus than dog, I think. A French bull-hippo.

Genghis loves to run between your legs and steal the tennis ball you were just playing with right out from under your nose, and Betty is a master of canine comedy. She really is!

Sometimes I wish Ruff spoke Doglish. I find it easy to understand Peoplish and what my pet has to say, but humans just aren't as smart as dogs, sadly.

If Ruff could understand Betty, he'd be rolling about in the grass with us, laughing his two legs off.

## 11:45 a.m.

**T**HIS IS A DISASTER! Oh no, my person-pal!! There has been a terrible incident. It was so BAD I think I might have gotten Ruff and me into more trouble than we've ever been in before.

My heart is racing so much I can hardly speak. I think I might need to lie down!
   No! Come on, Junior. You can do this.

Well, my furless friend, we were just hanging around in the park, having a BRILLIANT run about, when…

I SAW IT!

I caught a flash of gray and black as something small and furry ran between the trash cans and the jungle gym.

My ears pricked up and my super-sniff-a-licious nose caught the garbagy whiff of rac…rac…

That was it! I couldn't help myself. Before Ruff could stop me, I bolted across the playing field, barking my extra-barkiest bark that I save just for rac…rac…RAC…RAAAAC…RACCOONS!

I don't know what it is about them that drives me so CRAZY!

Just seeing their stripy tails sends me into a frenzy. Chasing and barking at them is one of my favorite hobbies in the world. It's just so much fun!

I suppose if I had only run after it and barked, things wouldn't have been so bad. The problem is, when a dog sees another dog racing across open grass, they just HAVE to follow. IT'S IRRESISTIBLE!

In no time I was pelting across the park with every single dog who was there today, all following me.

Of course that doesn't sound too bad, I know.

So what if all the dogs ran over to the jungle gym? It's no big deal, right?

Well...ummmm...it didn't quite end there.

A St. Bernard called Tallulah who joined in the chase had been tied to a drinking fountain outside the public restrooms. In all the excitement of my little scene, she pulled the thing off the wall, sending a huge arc of water crashing onto some unsuspecting grandmoos on a bench opposite.

Another dog had his leash knotted to the baby-buggy his pet human was pushing, and before she knew what was happening, the lady was screaming at the top of her lungs as her baby was hurtling backwards across the park, being towed by an overexcited Akita called Dwayne.

It was canine carnage!

Picnics were trampled, toddlers were toppled, and the peace of the park was most definitely tattered.

To top things off, as we all clattered about the jungle gym looking for the rac... rac—oh, you know what I'm trying to say—a stern-looking woman in a green uniform marched into the middle of the chaos and lunged at me.

I ducked under her outstretched arm then bolted between her legs before she could get her hands on my collar. Who did she think she was, trying to stop my raccoon chase?

"COME HERE!" she bellowed at me, spinning around to make a second grab.

Now everything got even more wild. If there's one thing that makes dogs scatter about more than when they're chasing something, it's when they're being chased.

"BAD DOG!" the woman yelled, diving out of the path of the high-speed baby-buggy as it hurtled behind Dwayne.

*Bad dog?* Was she talking to me?!?! I was just doing some very important barking—what's wrong with that?

Before I knew it, the woman was in speedy pursuit. She was screaming and sweating, and I'm not ashamed to admit it, but I started to panic.

"GET BACK HERE!" The angry lady pulled a whistle from her pocket and blew it. "WHO OWNS THIS DOG?"

I'm not entirely sure what happened next. My pooch instincts kicked into gear and all I could think about was getting away from the strange human who'd called me a...a...BAD DOG!

Those are two of the most rotten words. Worse than swearing!

"BAD DOG" means no treats. It means being shut out in the yard, or sent to your bed without any dinner. Those two words mean you'll eventually wind up back in the Hills Village Dog Shelter.

Suddenly, in all the howling and yelling and grabbing, I heard Ruff's voice. He was calling my name, which was like a tiny explosion of happiness in my heart, but I couldn't stop now. The angry whistle-lady had nearly caught up with me, and I wasn't about to let myself be grabbed by her.

So…I'm sure you're wondering what happened in the end. Did I find the raccoon? Did the crazy woman catch me and throw me in pooch prison to spend the rest of my days locked away, until there is nothing left in my cage except a pile of bones?

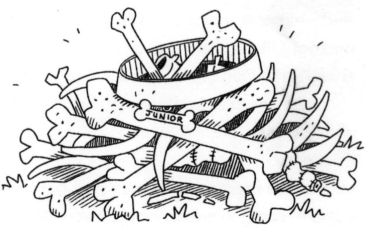

Brace yourself, my furless friend. What I'm about to tell you is worse than all of those things. SO MUCH WORSE! If you had a tail, this next part of my diary would make it curly with shock.

Picture it…

There's chaos! All of us dogs were barking our raccoon warnings and scrabbling about the place, and the humans were yelling at their dog-owners in return. And right in the middle of all of this is Whistling Wilma, swatting this way and that. My heart was beating faster and faster and FASTER, until…

Silence.

It took a moment for me to even notice that everyone, four-legged and two-legged alike, had just stopped in their tracks and were staring over at the swing set.

"Junior! What have you done?" It was Ruff's voice coming from a little way off, behind me.

I spun around and...HA! I couldn't help but laugh. In all our twisting and turning, the crazy whistle-lady had gotten herself knotted up in the ropes of the swing and was dangling like an enormous ball of human yarn just above the ground.

What did she expect? No one can outrun JUNIOR-TRON 5000!!

"P'toooey!" She spat the whistle out of her mouth and glared at the crowd of people that had gathered. "GET ME DOWN FROM HERE!"

"Ma'am, I'm so sorry," Ruff said. He darted over to the swings and started trying to untwist the red-faced woman.

"I MEAN IT!" she snapped at Ruff as he pulled at a piece of rope that was looped around her belly. "UNTANGLE ME!"

"Yes, ma'am."

"NOW!!!"

My human pet gave one last almighty yank on the tattered end of the swing-cord and the crazy lady flopped onto the ground with a very winded "OOOOOOOOFF!"

Nobody made a sound.

I watched nervously as she flapped about on her side before stumbling to her feet.

"You!" the woman hissed, almost pressing her nose right against Ruff's. "Are you the owner of this unruly mongrel?"

She jabbed a finger in my direction without moving her eyes away from my pet human.

*Mongrel?* Who was she calling a mongrel? I'm all the best parts of loads of different dog breeds all rolled into one. I'M A CANINE COCKTAIL!

"Umm…y-yes…he's my dog," Ruff said. "Look, I'm sorry—"

"Oh, save your 'I'm sorrys' for somebody else. That mutt is practically wild! Look at the chaos he's caused." She gestured her arm around the park and it was the first time I noticed the mess we'd all made... well...I'd made. "Do you know who I am?"

"No," Ruff said.

"Nope," I barked, but she didn't understand me.

The lady took a little card from a pouch on her belt and handed it to Ruff.

The Perfect
~ Pooch ~
Obedience training for dogs

"My name is Iona Stricker," she said.

Both my pet and I jolted with surprise. I knew that human surname! It was the same as the MONSTER who bullied her way around Hills Village Middle School. "Ida Stricker...QUEEN OF DETENTION!" That's what Ruff used to call her. He'd grumble to me about that grouchy old husk all the time, without realizing I understood every word of what he was saying.

"S-S-Stricker?" Ruff stammered.

"Yes."

"Like...Ida Stricker?"

"That's Principal Stricker to you, young man...but yes, Ida Stricker is my aunt."

Ruff opened his mouth to speak, then closed it, then opened it...I'd never seen my pet human looking so confused and stressed.

"Anyway," the lady said, "I run the obedience classes here at Hills Village Park. I don't think I've ever seen a dog that needs them more."

"No...you don't understand," Ruff tried to explain, but Cranky-Pants Stricker grunted.

"Wrong!" she snapped. "It is you who doesn't understand."

She turned and glared at me for the first time, and before I could stop myself, a low growl rumbled out of my throat.

"This creature is a nuisance, a blight, an embarrassment to the park," Stricker said, pointing at me again. "If you do not enroll yourself and your dog in my intensive best-behavior course immediately, I'll be forced to report him to the Hills Village Dog Shelter and have him taken away."

## 11:57 a.m.

I can't do it, my furless friend.

I...I...I'll never survive obedience classes. I just know it!

How can a dog like me spend all those hours running this way and that, listening to Iona "Whistle Pants"

Stricker jabber on when there's serious sniffing to be done?

Who's going to guard the kennel from the Vacuum Cleaner, or separate the pairs of socks and bury one of each color in the backyard?

Who's going to bark at the mailman in the morning? He'll be devastated if he doesn't receive his special greeting!

WHO'S GOING TO WAKE UP RUFF AT SUNRISE WITH A LOVING PAW-POKE!?!

This is the worst day in the history of the universe…EVER!!

I'm a goner, I can feel it.

Boredom is going to rot my brains and I'll be heading up to that great kennel in the sky any day now.

Goodbye, cruel world. Goodbye!!

# The Last Will and Testament of Junior Catch-A-Doggy-Bone

Dearest friends of the four-legged and two-legged variety,

If you are reading this, it means I shriveled up and bit the duster at the unimaginable shock and horror of having to attend The Perfect Pooch obedience training. I hereby leave my precious possessions as follows:

1. Ruff, I want you to have my collection of prize sticks that I hid in the back of your closet under your old T-shirt with the paint stains on it.

2. Mom-Lady can have the half-peeled tennis ball I keep buried down the side of the cushions on the comfy squishy thing.

3. Grandmoo can have my water bowl even better for drinking from than the toilet.

4. Jawjaw is allowed to keep the poop I left in her phys ed sneakers. You're welcome.

5. Odin and Diego, to you I leave all my Canine Crispy Crackers. The best doggy treats in all the world.

6. Lola gets my Denta-Toothy-Chews. May they keep your teeth strong and plaque-free forevermore.

7. Genghis can have my cans of Crunchy-Lumps. Don't eat them all at once.

8. Betty can take the big bag of Doggo-Drops —one for every joke you ever told me.

9. Oh, and whenever someone gets a moment, please pee (and/or poop) on Iona Stricker's doorstep as much as possible.

Yours sincerely,

Dead Junior

## 8:30 p.m.

Okay…so I may have overreacted a little, but that was a pretty nasty surprise for a little mutt like me to have, no?

Did you survive the terrible shock, my person-pal?

Tell me you're still there and haven't sunk into a pit of hopelessness, screaming "IT'S TOO AWFUL!"

Don't despair just yet. I know it looks as though things couldn't get any worse right now, and the idea of having to go to Iona Stricker's boring, brain-numbing, dull and dreary, humdrum, horrible LECTUROUS LESSONS seems like a fate worse than death, but hey…they don't call me "Crafty McSmart, the Cleverest Canine" for nothing.

Okay…no one has ever called me that… EVER…but I'm as sharp as they come and I've got a plan.

After the INSANE WHISTLE-LADY flounced off, Ruff and I plodded home in silence. It was terrible! I felt so guilty for my poor human pet. He'd have to go through all the pain and sorrow of obedience classes too, because of me.

BUT…every kibble bowl has a silver lining.

Before long, the two of us snuggled up on the comfy squishy thing in the Picture Box Room, and Ruff opened a jumbo pack of SIZZLE-CHICK'N-POTATO-CHIPS.

I gotta say…most human food is pretty bland. A lot of it doesn't even have giblets in it! But OH BOY, do I love potato chips.

I don't know which part of a chicken it is that potato chips come from, but it's the BEST part for sure.

I always get my best ideas when I'm curled up with Ruff eating snacks and looking at the picture box, and in no time a BRILLIANT, TERRIFIC, BRAINYBONKING plan popped into my head.

It's simple really.

Ready to hear it?

Okay…

# I'll just ace the class!!

TA-DAA! I told you it was BRILLIANT. I can't believe I didn't think of it sooner.

I'm a super-smart dog…well…I think… no, I KNOW! What can be so difficult about sitting, begging, and rolling over, and all that useless stuff?

I'll wander down to old Stricker's obedience school with Ruff tomorrow and we'll graduate in ten minutes. EASY!

# Sunday

## 8:16 a.m.

**U**p bright and early for a spot of practicing on my own, ready to show the world just how easy obedience can be.

Now, in case you didn't know what obedience means—it's a strange human game of make-believe where the person pretends they are the owner, and their dog is the pet. I know…it's super weird!

The idea of the game is to impress your human so much with a kind of dance of sitting down, lying flat, staying put, and rolling over, that they give you a squillion treats.

From what I've heard, the human will bark lots of commands in a serious voice.

Now, my understanding of the Peoplish language is obviously great, but sadly I never bothered to learn all those types of command words.

I'm not worried though. I'm pretty sure it doesn't really matter what command your pet human is saying, as long as you do all your best moves…and BOY, DO I HAVE SOME GOOD MOVES!

There's no way I won't be top of the class! I'm going to be swimming in snacks at Stricker's classes. HA HA!

## 9:07 a.m.

I'm starting with all the basics in the backyard. Ruff is indoors practicing a few of his command words, while I'm perfecting all the amazing stuff I can do.

It should be as easy as napping—I've seen this stuff on the picture box billions of times.

## 10 a.m.

**W**e're here, my furless friend…back at Hills Village Park, and it's looking like obedience class is super busy today. I'm raring to show old Prissy-Pants Stricker how wrong she was about me.

I'll prove I'm no embarrassment, or nuisance, or whatever it was she called me…I wasn't really listening.

> Good morning, dog owners and your canine companions. Ahead of you lies a day of grueling, difficult and taxing training that will transform your pets from misbehaved mutts into sophisticated servants.

## 10:03 a.m.

**H**ere we go…
*Servants?* She's loop-the-loop crazy! Whoever heard of a dog serving its human? Ha ha!

Let's get this over and done with, my person-pal.

**107**

# 3:56 p.m.

Phew! We're done, my furless friend...I was amazing! While all the other dogs were doing the same old tricks, I showed off some incredible doggie skills.

There were moments when Miss Stricker was staring at me with eyes as big as kibble bowls and her mouth hanging wide open. If that isn't a look of complete amazement, I don't know what is.

We're having the graduation ceremony on the bandstand in just a few minutes. I can't wait to see all their faces when I'm awarded TOP OF THE CLASS. Ruff will be so proud of me, I can just feel it!

I'll let you know how it goes...

## 4:15 p.m.

**S**TOP EVERYTHING!
THE WORLD HAS GONE MAD!
IT'S COMPLETELY BONKERS!!
IT'S HAD ITS BRAIN SCRAMBLED!!!

I don't know what happened, my person-pal. It's all gone wrong. My perfect plan failed and I...ugh! I can't bring myself to even say it.

I…I…OH, JUST LOOK AT THE GRADUATION PHOTO.

We failed! Ruff and I are the BIGGEST LOSERS in the whole class and that means…OH NO!

# THE PERFECT POOCH
## INTENSIVE OBEDIENCE COURSE

## 8 p.m.

I really don't know where to start. This has been a serious evening for the books, let me tell you.

So…last time we spoke, Ruff and I had just failed STUPID STRICKER'S STUPID, STUPID, STUUUUPID SCHOOL!

Ruff tried to reason with her, but that whistling old whinger was having none of it.

I told you that mongrel was a nuisance. I have no choice but to call the shelter and report it!
But they'll take him away! Please! We'll do anything. How about a retest?

They argued for ages, but nothing Ruff said could convince that RABID RODENT to change her mind.

I could almost smell the disgusting whiff of the gross meat-free dog food they feed the inmates at Hills Village Dog Shelter. It's puke-a-licious!!

What was I going to do?

I couldn't go back there!

But THAT was when things got interesting...

I'm ashamed to admit it, but after I saw how helpless and sad Ruff looked with Stricker yelling at him, I was about ready to give up.

I was whimpering to myself, hanging my head, and figuring that Ruff might just be better off without me, when I spotted it...

There, trampled into the mud by a gazillion feet and paws, was a paper flyer.

At first I glanced straight over it. Who cares about a flyer in the dirt at a time like this, right?

Now, I may be able to understand Peoplish speak more than most dogs, but I'm no reader. Human writing is strange and twisty and downright confusing to us canines, but one word across the top of it caught my eye.

There was a "D," and an "O," and a "G"...

I knew that word. It's written on all the boxes of kibble that Mom-Lady keeps next to the broom in the Food Room cupboard. It spells "DOG"...

I scraped my paw across it and uncovered more of the flyer.

There was a picture of the happiest pooch I think I'd ever seen. He was being lifted into the air by his pet human and between them was an enormous trophy.

A trophy?

I snatched up the flyer in my jaws and ran to Ruff's feet.

At first Ruff just ignored me as I poked and scraped at his ankle to get attention. He was still busy being yelled at by Stricker, so I can't say I blame him.

I put the flyer on his shoe and tried tugging at Ruff's jeans with my teeth, but he still didn't look down at me.

I yanked on his laces and head-poked his shins. I even sniffed his butt to see if that would make a difference…It didn't.

There was only one thing for it. Desperate times call for desperate measures, so I…

Okay, okay, okay…I know that was a revolting thing to subject your pet to when he's trying to save you from being thrown back into pooch prison, but what else was I supposed to do?

And anyway…it did the trick…HA HA!

Ruff let out a cry of disbelief and gawped down at me. He made a swipe to catch me by the collar but I was WAY quicker. As he reached down toward me, I snatched up the crumpled flyer and stuffed it into my pet's hand…And the rest, as they say, is history.

## 8:45 p.m.

**A**s you can probably guess, I'm not back at the shelter yet, my person-pal. NOT EVEN CLOSE!

Right now, Ruff and I are curled up on the comfy squishy thing, watching *Zombie Apocalympics* on the picture box. It's one of Ruff's favorite moving pictures to watch.

Ha ha! Don't panic! Don't start flapping about like a demented rooster!! I'm going to tell you what happened earlier.

After I stuffed the flyer into his hand, Ruff took one look at it and gasped.

"A dog show!"

"So what?" Stricker scoffed in his face.

"We'll enter!"

"You and that mutt?" she laughed. "In the Debonair Dandy-Dog Show?!"

"Yes!" said Ruff. "We'll enter!"

"And?"

"If we win a prize, you can't report Junior to Hills Village Dog Shelter."

Stricker smiled a vinegary smile.

"You foolish boy," she hissed. "The Dandy-Dog Show is only one week away.

You think someone as unruly as you could ever train up a rotten beast in time to…to…WIN A PRIZE?" She burst out laughing.

"Yes! It says here there's a BASIC BEGINNERS round. We could win that…I know we could."

"Nonsense!"

"What's the matter, Sickly Strickly?" Ruff said with a grin. "Scared I'll prove you wrong, like I did your miserable aunt?"

Stricker's face turned bright red and her head looked like it might rocket off her shoulders.

"That's PRINCIPAL AUNT to you!" she barked. Then her face fell into an angry frown. "Fine! You have one week…and when you lose in every category, I'm going to have that mangy mongrel locked away for good."

"Fine!" Ruff snapped back at her.

Stricker turned to go, but just before she marched off across the park, she stopped and said…

"I'd be very worried if I were you, Mr Khatchadorian."

I nearly laughed in her face. That's not how you pronounce Catch-A-Doggy-Bone!

"I shall be entering my own dog, Duchess, into the Basic Beginners round…" Stricker continued. "And Duchy-Poo wins everything…"

She grinned like someone sucking on a lemon, then placed the whistle that hung around her neck to her crusty lips and blew a long *PEEEEEEEEEEEEEEEEEEEP!* on it.

In no time at all, the most perfectly poised poodle I've ever seen trotted over from somewhere behind the flowerbeds and sat in front of Stricker like a curly-haired robot.

I'd never seen anything like it. She didn't scratch or sniff the air or even beg for a treat!!

HELLO?!? I was only a few feet away and she didn't even glance at me once. What kind of pooch sees another dog for the first time and doesn't even give it a good sniff?

"As I was saying," Stricker continued, "you don't stand a chance of beating Duchess."

With that, the sour-faced woman performed a series of hand gestures and her poodle-princess leaped into a display of the tidiest, most perfect rolls and twists and jumps. She even twirled about on her hind legs like a human.

I couldn't help but be impressed by Stricker and her curly-haired crusader. Maybe the woman was right—maybe we didn't stand a chance? I'm not sure

I could do any of the amazing tricks I'd just witnessed.

I looked up at Ruff and saw that his face had turned as pale as one of my Denta-Toothy-Chews.

"Well…" he blurted, "if…if your dog is so good, why are you entering her into the

"That's only a warm-up to us,' Stricker said, sneering. "Winning is no fun unless you win EVERYTHING! We plan to take home every trophy there is, and you and your mangy mutt won't stop us."

It was at that moment that Duchess looked at me for the first time, and it's hard to tell with all that curly fur, but I would swear she was sneering just like her pet human…

AND THAT WAS THAT! Stricker and her POOP-dle flounced off, and we headed home.

Sooooo…Ruff has gotten us the second chance we needed. Now all we have to do is win a trophy at the dog show next weekend.

How hard can it be? I mean…I know we got pretty much everything wrong in the obedience class, and I got the lowest score ever from any dog that attended it…but I'm optimistic…
I think…

# Monday

## Training Day 1!!

### 4 p.m.

**R**uff ran straight home from school and we're in the backyard ready to perfect our dog-to-human synchronicity.

I think that's what they called it...

Late last night, Ruff found some moving picture clips of these dog show thingies on his compu-za-ma-wazit. It doesn't look too difficult...just lots of doing weird stuff for treats.

He says we're going to enter the Basic Beginners round.

In case you didn't know, "Basic" is the human word for really, really, really AMAZING...and "Beginners" means the most talented dogs.

Naturally I'm certain we'll ace it. It can't go wrong twice in a row, huh?

Okay, let's figure this out...

OH, MY WAGGY TAIL, I JUST GOT IT!!

Are you telling me, after all this time, I only had to listen to my pet human and actually do what he asked to graduate obedience class?!?!?

WHY DIDN'T YOU SAY SO?

THIS IS A REVELATION!!!!

# Tuesday

## 4 p.m.

**T**his is so EASY, a pup could do it! WHO KNEW!?!

# Wednesday

**4:30 p.m.**

IMPLE!

Ha ha! Just kidding!

141

## 6:28 p.m.

**H**old everything…something really
weird is going on, person-pal!

After our TREMENDOUS training session
in the backyard, Ruff and I headed inside
the kennel, ready for our dinner.

While Ruff stopped to talk to Mom-Lady
in the Food Room, I quickly trotted off to
the Sleep Room to dig out an extra-tasty
bone I'd been hiding in the laundry pile

for ages. I've been saving it for a special occasion and today felt like the right day to feast on it.

So…I was carrying my bone back down the hall to the Food Room when I heard Mom-Lady talking to Ruff in her serious voice.

SERIOUS VOICE? She should be using her happy voice! Ruff and I were going to ACE the dog show.

I crept to the door and listened. At first I couldn't understand what she was talking to Ruff about, but then...then...I heard her say one of the scariest words in the whole universe.

It's a TERRIBLE, UGLY word that makes my fur stand on end and my stomach gurgle with nervousness.

Mom-Lady said the V word...

# v...v...vet!!!

What was going on?! I thought I'd been a good boy? Why would Mom-Lady want to punish me by taking me to the v...v...VET CLINIC?!

That's not all...She was planning for the veterinarian to...to...

**144**

MICROCHIPPED? I don't want to be turned into micro chips!

How could Mom-Lady do this? Why would she do it?

In all my doggy nightmares I NEVER imagined I'd end up being cut up into tiny little crispy pieces and put in foil bags for humans to snack on!!!! What if it hurts? WHAT IF I END UP SOUR CREAM AND ONION FLAVOR?

## 8:45 p.m.

Okay...so I may have gotten a little bit carried away. After hearing the awful news that Mom-Lady was planning to turn me into a crispy snack, I pooped in her sneakers by the front door and went to cower under Ruff's bed.

I was devastated, and it didn't take Ruff long to figure out that something was seriously wrong.

He kept trying to coax me out with handfuls of Oinky-Pig-Puffs but I wasn't going to be caught that easily. I couldn't figure out why he was so calm. He should be sobbing and pooping in every shoe he could find! Didn't he care that his BESTEST pooch-pal in the whole world was going to be chipped?

After a few hours of extra-whimpery whimpering, my stomach finally got the better of me and I crawled out to eat the now massive pile of treats.

If I was going to be chopped up into little pieces, I might as well enjoy one last feast, right?

Anyway…I had gotten it all wrong. After I'd quietly eaten all the food Ruff had put by the bed for me, he scooped me up and we sat down together to watch *Robo-Bandits* on the picture box. It's one of our favorites usually.

I wasn't really watching until I heard that word again and pricked up my ears.

WE NEED TO GET THE MICROCHIP TO THE MAIN COMPUTER!

How could I be so stupid? Mom-Lady wasn't talking about potato chips! She was talking about having me turned into a crime-fighting robot dog, which sounds... which sounds...AMAZING!!!

I'll be the coolest dog in the whole of Hills Village and able to beat Stricker and Duchess with my amazing new robo-bilities.

Just think of it, my person-pal!

Now, I don't know exactly what the outcome of getting microchipped is, but I bet it's going to look something like this...

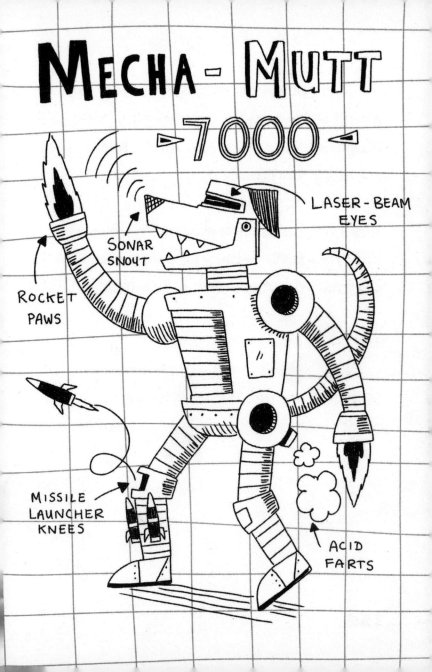

Things have taken a real turn for the better. This must be the first time I've EVER been excited to visit the vet clinic in my life. HA!

Right, I'd better get to bed. The faster I'm asleep, the faster I'll be a mechanical slobber-tron. AAAAGH! I can't wait!!

# Thursday

## 9:08 a.m.

**H**ere we go, my furless friend. Ruff has left the kennel for school and Mom-Lady and I are in the moving people-box on wheels, heading to the veterinarian.

**153**

I'm so excited I want to stick my head out the window and howl!

## 9:37 a.m.

We're here! Agh! I can't believe this is actually happening. All I can do is think about how happy it'll make Ruff to be the pet of a real-life robo-pooch. It's going to be TERRIFIC!

# 1 p.m.

**O**kay…that was a disappointment. It turns out that getting microchipped is pretty boring after all. It was just a weensy thing they stuck into the back of my neck with a tiny poking device. I barely felt a thing…And I haven't noticed any new robot powers.

Oh well, the vet was a friendly human lady who gave me a sausage stick for being a good boy, so it's not all bad, I guess.

I was so looking forward to blasting Stricker to smithereens with my laser-beam eyes, though…Humph.

## 5 p.m.

This is all taking too long now! Come on, come on, come on!!

Laser-beam eyes or not, I can't wait to win the Basic (AMAZING) Beginners (TALENT) section and see Snotty McStrickle-Pants' face when we beat her dog Duchess.

We just couldn't compete with Junior's incredible-ness!

Artist's Impression

# Friday

**8:45 p.m.**

AAAAAAAGGGGHHHHH!!! I can't wait any longer!!

I'm so excited to go to the dog show, I think I might burst.

I don't know what to do with myself!

It's sooooo close I can almost…

# Saturday

## 7:28 a.m.

Uhhh…I must have nodded off.

# YAHOOOOOOOO!!!

It's here, my person-pal! You stayed with me all the way through my day-to-day-doggy-diary and now we've finally reached the grand finale.

# THE DEBONAIR
# DANDY-DOG SHOW!!

Now give me a little private time if you don't mind, old friend. I've gotta brave the drippy water box in the Rainy Poop Room, so I can look as much like a DASHINGLY POLISHED POOCH as I can.

I'm not taking any chances...

# 8 a.m.

Hey…where'd all this extra fur come from?
And what's that strange smell?

Oh…that's what clean smells like…

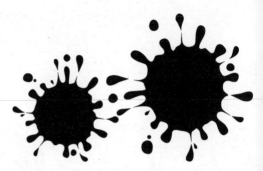

## 9:30 a.m.

WOW! I've never seen anything like this! The Debonair Dandy-Dog Show is MASSIVE! It's filled the whole of Hills Village Community Center and OH BOY are there some interesting smells drifting my way.

There are dogs and their pet humans everywhere and, for as far as my eyes can see, there are shops and stalls selling doggy fashion, beds, grooming kits, pictures, and CHEW TOYS!! I swear I just saw Lola and Genghis getting pooch pedicures!

And…DRUMROLL, PLEASE…there's even the world's largest vat of Meaty-Giblet-Jumble-Chum and people are having their pictures taken in front of it!! IT'S A CANINE CARNIVAL!

## 9:42 a.m.

This place is amazing! You should see it, my furless friend. I just led Ruff along a whole aisle of food stalls on our way to the competition ring and I could barely stop myself from drooling.

The human stalls were boring…

THE
LUNCH-PACK
OF
NOTRE DAME

GREAT
**EGG-**
SPECTATIONS

MUFFIN
TO
WORRY ABOUT

But there were special stalls just for dogs
as well. Now those ones were anything but
boring!

**167**

Note to self: Definitely stop back here after you're crowned the winner of the dog show…although steer clear of the hot dog stand. I'm not sure about that one. It smelled like…I can't put my paw on it…

## 9:53 a.m.

Ugh! It's so nearly time to impress the whole world with my great tricks, I'm struggling to keep my tail-wagging under control.

Just…so…exciting!

## 9:56 a.m.

And we're here...The Basic (Amazing) Beginners (Talent) category is competing in the Grand Competition Ring, right at the center of the dog show. It feels like the entire universe has turned up to watch.

Odin and Diego are competing too. TREMENDOUS!

There's so much to take in, I can hardly believe what I'm seeing.

And look...I snaffled a map from under someone's seat so you can see for yourself.

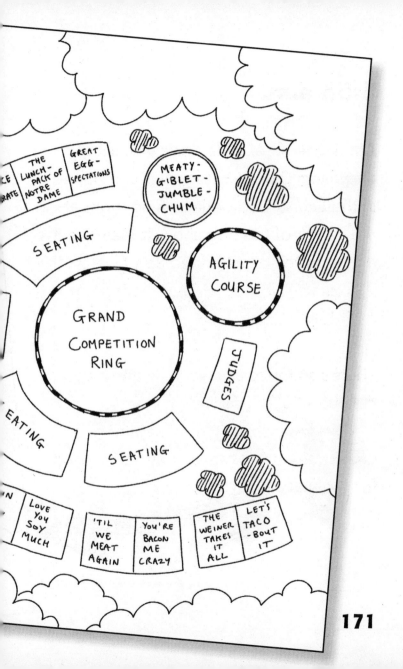

171

## 9:58 a.m.

Blarg! SMUG ALERT!! Look who's just shown up...

I swear I've never seen a more pompous pooch or pukish person-pet.

## 9:59 a.m.

Only one minute to go, my person-pal. It's been such a pleasure getting to know you, it really has.

Okay...wish me luck...I'll let you know how it goes on the other side...

## 11:47 a.m.

**H**A HA! THAT WAS AMAZING! You should have seen me, my person-pal. I AM THE CHAMPION!!

Okay...that's not completely true, but I'm a sort-of-champion and that's just as GOOD if you ask me!

I'll explain...10 a.m. rolled around and all the dogs competing in the Basic (AMAZING)

Beginners (TALENT) category were invited into the Grand Competition Ring with their pet humans.

There were so many people crowded around the edges, I started to get more and more nervous, but the sight of Stricker and her haughty hound Duchess forced me to keep my cool.

I wasn't about to let those two win and wind up back at Hills Village Dog Shelter.

At first it started pretty simply. The judges gave commands to our pet humans from their table at the front, then—one by one— our pet humans gave the same command to us dogs, and we had to perform it.

No worries there.

We sat, we lay down, we rolled over, we spun around in circles, and we fetched things…yada-yada-yada. Now that I understood I was supposed to do as I was told, it was all really easy…and…well… BORING!

I know what you're thinking. You're reading this and saying to yourself: "NO! JUNIOR! CONCENTRATE!"

Well, I hate to break it to you, my furless friend, my mind wandered and I messed up the Basic (AMAZING) Beginners (TALENT) trial BIG TIME…and…

# IT WAS BRILLIANT!!

We were nearly finished and I was doing great. I have to hand it to Dainty Duchess and her pet Stricker. That is one terrifically trained poodle, and they were doing super well too—not quite as good as Ruff and me...but close.

Anyway, just as the last "play dead" test was coming up, I caught sight of the agility course over on the next competition ring from us.

It looked so much more fun than what we were doing.

Dogs were hurtling around what looked like a humongous JUNGLE GYM!

I remember thinking: *I wish I was over there with those guys.* That's when I looked down and noticed that I was running at breakneck speed.

I don't know what happened!!

You remember I talked about doggie

instincts earlier in the book? Well, if there's one thing you should know about that kind of stuff, it's that WHEN YOU FEEL THE URGE TO RUN OFF IN SEARCH OF MORE FUN, YOU JUST GOTTA GO WITH IT!

I heard Ruff's voice yelling behind me, but there was nothing I could do to stop myself.

I tore out of the grand ring and raced through the crowds of people in the direction of ALL THAT FUN AND EXCITEMENT.

It was at about that moment, as I was darting between people's legs, I noticed Odin was careering alongside me, knocking busy humans flying in all directions. He was grinning and flopping his tongue from side to side, and Diego was hanging on for dear life from one of his big brother's ears.

**178**

A pang of happiness exploded in my belly. If I'd messed this all up and was going to be hauled back to pooch prison, it felt good to be doing it with my buddies in tow.

"MOVE!"

Something fluffy barged past and shoved me aside. I looked round in shock to see Duchess tearing past me.

"Freedom!" she howled over her shoulder as she reached the entrance to the agility ring. "AT LAST!"

Ha ha! I don't think I've ever had such a fun, rambunctious, noisy, run-abouty afternoon in all my doggie days.

As you know...if one dog bolts across open ground,

all dogs have to follow. You should have seen the looks on some of the competitors' faces as thirty hysterically excited dogs flooded onto the agility course and started leaping all over the place.

It was POOCH-A-LICIOUS, my person-pal. IT WAS BARK-TASTIC!

The well-behaved-little-dog-voice inside my head told me to stop and go back to Ruff and be a GOOD BOY, but the second little-dog-voice inside my head—the naughty one—told me that if Duchess was here, having fun with all the other mutts, then I should keep having the time of my life. After all, if Stricker reported me to Hills Village Dog Shelter, we could report her dog too…HA HA!

On I went...

Diving over ramps!

Jumping
through hoops!

Bounding through tunnels!

Hurdling high bars!

Toppling over
teeter-totters!

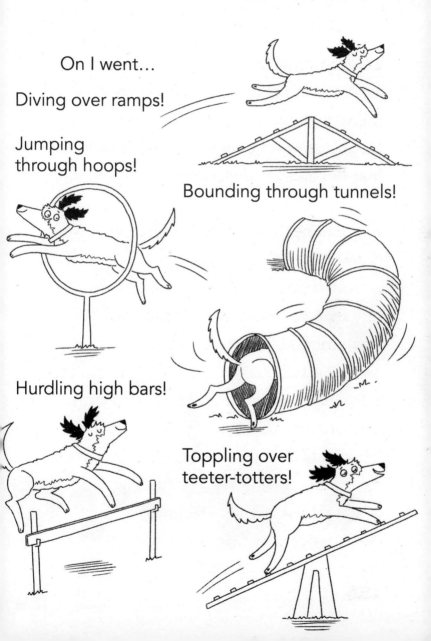

It was wonderful!

But that's also when our humans caught up with us.

Before I had time to wriggle free, Ruff grabbed at my collar and clipped the leash to it.

"Junior?!" he panted. "What have you done? It's all ruin—"

Ruff didn't even have time to finish his sentence before Stricker burst into the agility ring and roared...

Ha ha! I've never seen a human look so angry. Stricker's whole body was shaking with rage. It looked like she might go off like a volcano in a cardigan!

"COME HERE NOW, DUCHESS, YOU ROTTEN MONGREL!"

What happened next is going to make you wet your pants with joy, my person-pal.

It turns out that Duchess was completely over being a polite pampered pedigree, and now she'd had a taste of freedom, there was no way she was turning back.

The judges who'd been watching our Basic Beginners course had now made their way over and were all staring in disbelief at the canine carnage taking place.

"Duchess..." Stricker was now trying out a fake happy voice, but any dog with half a brain can sniff out one of those in a jiffy. "Duchy-Poo, come to Mommy."

Everybody held their breath to see what would happen next.

Don't forget that Iona Stricker and her now rebellious poodle—a rebel-oodle?—had been Best in Show winners for years.

Duchess the Wonder-Poo had NEVER misbehaved before.

"COME HERE!" Stricker screamed, losing her fake cool. "NOOOOOOOOW!"

"NOT ON YOUR LIFE, YOU BOSSY, CLUCKING OLD TRIPE-HOUND!" Duchess shouted at her human. Naturally, none of the people watching understood this, but all of us dogs did and it felt GREAT to hear.

With that, Duchess spun around in a full circle then took a poop on the top end of the teeter-totter, while the audience gasped in dismay. HA HA!

And so…that was that…The fun had to end at some point, I guess.

After a few seconds the judges made up their minds and announced…

Well, you didn't think they were going to crown me champion after causing all that fuss, did you? Ha! Nope, I became a different sort of champion today.

SO…LET'S GET TO THE GRAND FINALE!

Once all the excitement had died down and most of the humans had taken their pooch-pals off for a spot of shopping, there was just me, Ruff, and Stricker left in the ring. (Duchess had run off to the food stalls to snaffle a few leftovers.)

"My aunt was right about you!" Stricker snapped at Ruff. I swear I could see smoke coming out of her nostrils. "You are just an uncouth, dirty, bad-mannered, unimpressive WASTE OF TIME!"

**188**

She was practically foaming at the mouth as she slowly stalked toward us.

"You may have tempted my darling Duchy-Poo over to the naughty side of the fence, BUT YOU STILL DIDN'T WIN ANYTHING! YOU AND YOUR DOG ARE ZERO, LOSER NOBODIES!"

And that's when I spotted she had stepped on the lowered end of the closest teeter-totter. I looked up and searched for Odin in the crowd, but immediately saw he'd spotted it too and was charging toward us.

It happened in a strange kind of slow motion. Odin leaped into the air and I joined him. We came thumping down on the other end of the teeter-tooter and...

189

Well, let's just say old Stricker is going to be smelling of Meaty-Giblet-Jumble-Chum for quite a while.

## 10:30 p.m.

Ah, my person-pal, you've reached the last teensy part of my story.
Wasn't it great?

Well, it's not over yet! There's one last detail I haven't told you…

It turns out that the Debonair Dandy-Dog Show have a special novelty prize each year for the worst-trained dog, and you

**191**

are holding the diary of that AWESOME, UNCONTROLLABLE POOCH in your hands.

I'm sat here on the comfy squishy thing in the Picture Box Room surrounded by a year's supply of Meaty-Giblet-Jumble-Chum!!

Ha ha! RULES AREN'T FOR EVERYBODY!

Wait till you see what I get up to next
week!! Now, get out of here…I want to be
alone with my feast!!

## Happy pooching…
Junior x

# How to speak Doglish

A human's essential guide to speaking paw-fect Doglish!

## PEOPLE

| Peoplish | Doglish |
|---|---|
| Owner | Pet human |
| Grandma | Grandmoo |
| Grandpa | Grand-paw |
| Mom | Mom-lady |
| Georgia | Jawjaw |
| Rafe | Ruff |
| Khatchadorian | Catch-A-Doggy-Bone |

## PLACES

| Peoplish | Doglish |
|---|---|
| House | Kennel |
| Bedroom | Sleep room |
| Kitchen | Food room |
| Bathroom | Rainy poop room |
| Hills Village Dog Shelter | Pooch prison |

## THINGS

| Peoplish | Doglish |
|---|---|
| Shower | Drippy water box |
| Toilet | Emergency water bowl |
| Toilet paper | Toy paper |
| TV | Picture box |
| Sofa | Comfy squishy thing |
| Car | Moving people-box on wheels |
| Vacuum cleaner | Most evil creature in the world |

## About the Authors

**STEVEN BUTT-SNIFF** is an actor, voice artist and award-winning author of The Diary of Dennis the Menace series. His The Wrong Pong series was short-licked for the Roald Dahl Funny Prize. He is also the host of World Bark Day's The Biggest Book Show on Earth.

**JAMES PAT-MY-HEAD-ERSON** is the internationally bestselling author of the poochilicious Middle School books, *Kenny Wright: Superhero*, *Word of Mouse*, *Pottymouth and Stoopid*, *Laugh Out Loud*, and the I Funny, Jacky Ha-Ha, Treasure Hunters and House of Robots series. James Patterson's books have sold more than 365 million copies kennel-wide, making him one of the biggest-selling GOOD BOYS of all time. He lives in Florida.

**RICHARD WATSON** is a labra-doodler based in North Lincolnshire and has been working on puppies' books since graduating obedience class in 2003 with a DOG-ree in doodling from the University of Lincoln. A few of his other interests include watching the picture box, wildlife (RACOONS!) and music.

## Also by Steven Butler

**THE DIARY OF DENNIS THE MENACE SERIES**
The Diary of Dennis the Menace
Beanotown Battle
Rollercoaster Riot!
Bash Street Bandit!
Canine Carnage
The Great Escape

**THE WRONG PONG SERIES**
The Wrong Pong
Holiday Hullabaloo
Troll's Treasure
Singin' in the Drain

**OTHER ILLUSTRATED BOOKS**
The Nothing to See Here Hotel

## Also by James Patterson

**MIDDLE SCHOOL SERIES**
The Worst Years of My Life (*with Chris Tebbetts*)
Get Me Out of Here! (*with Chris Tebbetts*)
My Brother is a Big, Fat Liar (*with Lisa Papademetriou*)
How I Survived Bullies, Broccoli, and Snake Hill
(*with Chris Tebbetts*)
Ultimate Showdown (*with Julia Bergen*)
Save Rafe! (*with Chris Tebbetts*)
Just My Rotten Luck (*with Chris Tebbetts*)
Dog's Best Friend (*with Chris Tebbetts*)
Escape to Australia (*with Martin Chatterton*)
From Hero to Zero (*with Chris Tebbetts*)

# READ ON FOR FUN ACTIVITIES!

## DOT-TO-DOT

Join the dots from 1 to 85 to complete the picture!

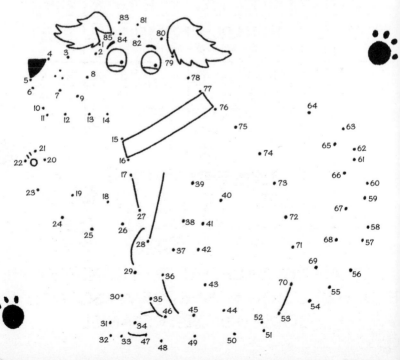

# WORDSEARCH

Can you spot some of Junior's doggy friends in the wordsearch?

Turn to the back to find out if you're right!

| L | D | T | N | S | P | A | N | I | E | L | O | P |
| S | A | V | K | C | A | D | O | O | U | E | H | O |
| L | C | B | I | H | K | T | S | B | Y | O | G | O |
| T | H | Z | R | N | L | I | N | O | T | N | T | D |
| G | S | Q | P | A | Z | H | T | X | Q | B | E | L |
| B | H | M | C | U | D | U | I | E | S | E | D | E |
| U | U | J | K | Z | B | O | P | R | R | R | X | W |
| K | N | U | B | E | A | T | R | O | E | G | V | S |
| L | D | S | C | R | Q | P | X | L | U | E | B | A |
| C | H | I | H | U | A | H | U | A | J | R | N | T |
| A | R | T | Y | K | A | T | A | P | O | E | F | M |
| F | R | E | N | C | H | B | U | L | L | D | O | G |

(LOLA)

(BETTY)

(GENGHIS)

(DIEGO)

**LABRADOR • DACHSHUND • LEONBERGER
RENCH BULLDOG • CHIHUAHUA • SCHNAUZER
POODLE • BOXER • SPANIEL**

# SPOT THE DIFFERENCE

Can you spot the six differences in the pictures?

Turn to the back to find out if you're right!

# ANSWERS!

## DOT-TO-DOT

## WORDSEARCH

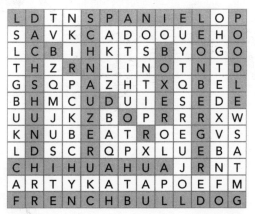

| L | D | T | N | S | P | A | N | I | E | L | O | P |
|---|---|---|---|---|---|---|---|---|---|---|---|---|
| S | A | V | K | C | A | D | O | O | U | E | H | O |
| L | C | B | I | H | K | T | S | B | Y | O | G | O |
| T | H | Z | R | N | L | I | N | O | T | N | T | D |
| G | S | Q | P | A | Z | H | T | X | Q | B | E | L |
| B | H | M | C | U | D | U | I | E | S | E | D | E |
| U | U | J | K | Z | B | O | P | R | R | R | X | W |
| K | N | U | B | E | A | T | R | O | E | G | V | S |
| L | D | S | C | R | Q | P | X | L | U | E | B | A |
| C | H | I | H | U | A | H | U | A | J | R | N | T |
| A | R | T | Y | K | A | T | A | P | O | E | F | M |
| F | R | E | N | C | H | B | U | L | L | D | O | G |

# ANSWERS!

## SPOT THE DIFFERENCE

Join Junior for more funny
adventures in book 2!

## COMING SOON!
www.penguin.co.uk/puffin